FAST EDDIE

Fast Eddie

by Janet Wyman Coleman
pictures by Alec Gillman

Four Winds Press ✳ New York

Maxwell Macmillan Canada Toronto
Maxwell Macmillan International
New York Oxford Singapore Sydney

Text copyright © 1993 by Janet Wyman Coleman
Illustrations copyright © 1993 by Alec Gillman
All rights reserved. No part of this book may be reproduced or
transmitted in any form or by any means, electronic or mechanical,
including photocopying, recording, or by any information storage
and retrieval system, without permission in writing from the Publisher.

Four Winds Press
Macmillan Publishing Company
866 Third Avenue
New York, NY 10022
Maxwell Macmillan Canada, Inc.
1200 Eglinton Avenue East
Suite 200
Don Mills, Ontario M3C 3N1
Macmillan Publishing Company is part of the
Maxwell Communication Group of Companies.
First edition
Printed and bound in the United States of America
10 9 8 7 6 5 4 3 2 1
The text of this book is set in Goudy Catalogue.
The illustrations are rendered in Prismacolor pencil.
Book design by Andrea Schneeman

Library of Congress Cataloging-in-Publication Data
Coleman, Janet Wyman.
Fast Eddie / by Janet Wyman Coleman ; pictures by Alec Gillman. — 1st ed.
    p.   cm.
Summary: To the dismay of Puff the cat and Jones the squirrel,
Fast Eddie the raccoon takes on his human neighbors one final time.
ISBN 0-02-722815-0
[1. Raccoons—Fiction.   2. Cats—Fiction.   3. Animals—Fiction.]
I. Gillman, Alec, ill.   II. Title.
PZ7.C67713Fas   1993
[Fic]—dc20   92-31243

Dedicated to
Ruth and Frank,
my three men,
and great friends,
without whom
Ed and Puff
would never have seen
the light of day

—J. W. C.

It took place in the suburbs. Not on some beaming mountainside or at the edge of a slurping lake. It could have happened in California, Maine, or even New Jersey . . . anyplace where there are people and trash.

1

At THE END of the driveway, two animals faced each other. The sun was setting behind them, so you couldn't make out their features. There were pointed ears, round noses, and whiskers. One animal had a long tail. It lay on the tar like a dead snake. The other had a short, wispy tail.

"You're new around here, aren't you?" It was the velvet voice of a cat.

The red squirrel nodded. He noticed the cat had a permanent smile.

"Have you met Eddie?"

The squirrel thought it was an odd question. "No, I haven't," he said.

"The raccoon. You must have heard of him."

"No. I haven't," the squirrel repeated. *This one's not a fighter,* he decided. *No scratches and her fur is clean and white.*

The cat's ear flicked. She leaned forward and whispered, "Wait a minute! You've never heard of Fast Eddie? I can't believe it."

A pair of barn swallows exploded from the garage. They dipped and flew straight toward the squirrel and the cat. At the last second, the birds swooped into a maple tree.

A hundred yards away, a raccoon headed toward his hole. His fur glistened. A magnificent tail floated behind him. In an old oak tree, two crows watched his progress.

"I won't miss him a bit when they finally get him," chuckled the first crow.

"Me neither," agreed the other.

The raccoon vanished, as if the earth had swallowed him whole.

A gust of wind wiped the field, knocking the tall grass backward. It circled the pine trees and shook the top branches. A single cloud meandered across the sky.

2

A SCREEN DOOR squeaked. The squirrel hopped behind the tire of the station wagon and squatted in the shadow.

"Kitty! Here, Kitty!"

The cat licked her shoulder until a square patch of wet fur appeared.

"Come on, Kitty! Dinner!"

The squirrel peered around the tire. He inspected the Victorian house and the attached barn. It was a purple-gray, like the sky in winter, but the trim was as white as milkweed. There were large windows and square porches with flat roofs. Jones loved flat roofs. The clapboards, he noticed, looked like telephone wires. They circled the house, connecting the windows. His eyes focused on a woman.

"Dinner!" Blond curls surrounded the woman's face. She wore a purple T-shirt and baggy blue jeans. Her toes curled over the porch steps.

"Hurry up!" The head of broccoli resting in her hands looked like a bridal bouquet.

The cat lifted her head and smoothed it against the chrome bumper. "That's Mrs. Plotkin," she said. "She loves gardens and pink things. You should see the chairs in the living room."

"Kitty! Here, Kitty!"

"Who's Kitty?" the squirrel whispered.

There was a noise in the woods. A golden retriever thrashed through the trees, kicking dead leaves high in the air. Her tongue dangled from her open mouth. The dog erupted from the trees and raced across the lawn. Her ears blew straight back. She veered around the station wagon, brushing her shoulder on the fender. The squirrel recoiled from the dog's four galloping legs. The dog gulped for air and sat at Mrs. Plotkin's feet. Her tail swept back and forth.

"Where have you been? I'll bet you've been in the trash next door." A pink tongue reached for the broccoli. Mrs. Plotkin lifted it above her shoulder.

"That's Kitty," the cat said. "Mrs. Plotkin named her that. Mr. Plotkin doesn't think it's funny."

"Go on in, you silly dog. Time for your second meal." The screen door whined and slammed.

The cat ducked under the car, too. She crouched and rolled onto her back. Her eyes moved across the oil pan to the tail pipe to the end of the driveway. She watched a car drive by upside down.

"Names are so important," the cat said. "I wanted to be called Samantha, but the Plotkins named me Puff. Imagine being called Puff! I always thought I'd be famous, but you can't be famous with a name like that." The cat scowled. "By the way, what's your name?"

"Jones." The squirrel cleared his throat. "Jones," he repeated, but he was thinking, *Why would anyone want to be famous?*

"What?"

"Jones."

"Jones what?"

"Just Jones."

"Where'd you get a name like that?"

"Off a mailbox," the squirrel replied. "When Mother ran out of names, she took them off mailboxes."

"Oh," said the cat. Her head twisted toward the house. "Do you like porches?" she asked.

"Just porch roofs."

"You mean you've never slept on a porch?"

The squirrel shook his head.

"You have to find one with a triangle of sunlight." The cat closed her eyes. "You lie down so that the sun falls on your stomach. Your fur gets warm and then hot. There's no better feeling. You stretch as far as you can. You pretend to be asleep, but actually you're listening. First, you hear big noises, like trucks. After a while, you hear everything. Yesterday, there were two mosquitoes arguing. One wanted to go inside and the other one didn't." The cat's tail lifted, twitched, paused, and drifted to the tar.

The squirrel tiptoed around the tire. "What's in there?" he asked. His brown eyes fastened to the barn. Puff rolled onto her side. Bits of leaves stuck to her fur.

"The barn?" the cat replied. "It has high spots for sitting and looking down. You'd like that, Jones. There are tunnels underneath. They lead to the cellar. On the hottest day, it's cold in the barn. It smells of horses and chickens."

"Nice pine." The squirrel admired the large tree next to the barn door.

"I hate pines," Puff groaned. "The sap gets stuck in my fur. It takes me days to lick it out and I can't stand the taste."

"My brother was saved by a pine tree," Jones said. "He slipped on a wet roof and somersaulted backward. A branch reached out and grabbed him. He said it was like falling into grass clippings." Jones took a deep breath and scampered across the driveway.

"Where are you going?" Puff yelled.

At the base of the pine tree, the squirrel hesitated. His eyes followed the trunk to the gutter. He crouched and jumped straight up.

I wonder how he avoids the sap, Puff thought.

In the middle of the tree, a branch jerked. It

dropped to the roof, depositing the squirrel on the black shingles.

Sammy Plotkin stood at his bedroom window, holding two plastic dinosaurs. He made a noise and slammed the figures together. Sammy smiled and glanced out the window. On the top of the barn roof, he noticed a squirrel. The animal was so still, it didn't look real.

"Mom," Sammy yelled, "can we get a weather vane someday?"

Mrs. Plotkin had just turned on the dishwasher, so she didn't hear the question.

3

"I WISH WE could plant corn out back again, Sandra."

Mr. Plotkin stood at the dining room window, staring at a field of ragweed and goldenrod. He was a gangly man. He looked like he'd been stretched and hadn't snapped back. His eyebrows connected in the middle behind tortoiseshell glasses. On Saturdays, he always wore a plaid shirt. It was rolled up above the elbows, exposing arms dotted with white paint.

Mrs. Plotkin stepped in front of her husband and closed the window halfway. Her arms were soft and graceful, but there was a smudge of dirt on each elbow.

"I wish I could have talked the farmer into it," Mr. Plotkin continued, "but he says it's not worth the effort, with the raccoons destroying all the corn."

Mrs. Plotkin crossed her arms. "I love the wild-flowers," she said, "especially at this hour. The yellow blossoms seem the brightest just before the sun goes down."

Mr. Plotkin's fingers raked through his brown hair. He pushed the glasses up his nose. "The goldenrod's coming down. I'm mowing it this weekend. I'm sick of sneezing and waking up with swollen eyes." He glared at his wife. "That's not supposed to be a garden. It's a cornfield."

Mr. Plotkin's hands gripped his belt. "I loved watching that corn grow," he sighed. "Don't you remember? In July, it was Sammy's height. By the end of August, it was 'as high as an elephant's eye.' "

Mrs. Plotkin twisted the pearl in her left ear.

"Those raccoons are ordinary vandals," Mr. Plotkin went on. "They make a mess out of everything. They're no better than the teenagers who steal stop signs and hit our mailbox with a baseball bat. And who ends up paying for it? We do! We always pay for it in the end."

"Come on, George," Mrs. Plotkin said. "Raccoons are just hungry."

"Sandra, we're not talking about six-hundred-pound raccoons. Hunger doesn't explain why they

destroy the whole field. They eat what they need and vandalize the rest. Take my word for it!"

"Well, how do other farmers deal with the raccoon problem?" Mrs. Plotkin gazed up at her husband. There was an expression on his face that she'd never seen before.

Mr. Plotkin turned away. "They shoot them," he said.

Four other eyes watched the swaying blossoms. Jones sat in the gutter. Puff crouched on the woodpile.

The squirrel scanned the landscape. *Great trees,* he thought. *Close enough together. No big jumps.* He admired the jungle gym and the smooth lawn. He pulled his tail under him. *Comfortable gutters. Soft and deep. There's really nothing like an old wooden gutter.*

Puff closed her eyes and listened. "Crickets," she said. "So many crickets." She heard a mouse chewing below her and a beetle stuck on his back, complaining. In the maple tree, the chickadees were singing songs of summer. "With trees at your feet, and wind beneath your wings," they sang.

Jones looked down at the cat. "You're so white," he said. "It must be hard to hide."

"It is. The two gray spots help a little. They came from my mother. She was Siamese. That's why I have light blue eyes. She was amazing, Jones. My mother had a meow that you could hear for miles."

"No kidding," Jones said.

"My father really had trouble hiding," Puff went on. "He was totally white. He had quite a reputation, though. I've been told he was the most elegant cat in town. When he moved, he looked like he was on ice skates."

Jones shuddered. "I hate ice," he said. "It makes the wires and gutters so treacherous. I've lost a lot of friends to ice. What happened to your parents?"

"I don't know," said Puff. "The Plotkins took me away from them when I was small. Sometimes I wonder if they're still alive. Eddie says it's better not to know. His mother was killed by a car at the end of the driveway. He saw the whole thing."

"Really?" said Jones.

"I can't believe you've never heard of Fast Eddie. He's so famous." Puff sat back on her hind legs. She lifted her paw and inspected the pads.

"Why's he famous?" the squirrel asked.

The cat's claws spread apart and she chewed the fur between them. She licked the side of her paw three times. Her eyes closed and her chin sank to her chest. The clean paw scooped into her ear. She

hoped to dig out a flea. She licked the paw again and placed it on the woodpile.

"Everybody's heard of Fast Eddie," the cat said, "because he's done so many things. He can knock down bird feeders and twist lids off jars. Once he got cottage cheese and chocolate pudding out of the trash and finger painted on the garage door. His artichoke leaf sculptures are amazing. Some of the birds think he's sick, but Eddie says they just don't understand what it means to be a raccoon."

"He's a friend of yours?" Jones asked.

Puff nodded. "Not just a regular friend. As Eddie's always reminding me, he's my best friend."

"But I thought cats were neat," the squirrel said.

Puff looked up at the gutter. "Are all your friends just like you?"

Jones thought for a minute and said, "Yes."

"Well, mine aren't. Kitty drools, but she's a friend. And Eddie. Well, Eddie's messy and he's dangerous, but he's a friend, too."

Puff's head dropped back, exposing a long, downy neck. "Oh, look, Jones," she said. "It's the first star! Let's see. What am I going to wish for? Come on, Jones. You've got to make a wish!"

"Wish for lamb chop bones and orange rinds," said a voice from the bottom of the woodpile.

4

RED SQUIRRELS PRIDE themselves on their great hearing. They can hear a fly turn a corner. The best red squirrels can tell the difference between the chew of a carpenter ant and that of a termite. However, Jones never heard Fast Eddie coming.

"Wish for stale Halloween candy, while you're at it," the raccoon added. "But whatever you do, don't wish for Chinese food."

Jones lifted out of the gutter, flailed at the roof, and vanished. A masked face appeared behind Puff's tail. "Who was that?" the raccoon asked.

"Jones."

Fast Eddie pulled himself up on the woodpile. He sat back on his haunches and searched the roof and gutters. Puff squatted and curled her paws into her chest.

The raccoon's fur was radiant and fluffy. A flawless tail with seven perfectly spaced rings rested behind him. A black mask as dark as the deepest corner of a cellar surrounded his eyes. Puff loved Eddie's brown eyes. They weren't small and expressionless like most raccoon eyes. They were the size of large strawberries and they looked like they could laugh all by themselves.

"Jones," Eddie repeated. "He'd heard of me?"

"Nope."

The striped tail jerked. "Really? Where'd he come from?"

"He didn't say. Awful name, don't you think?"

"By the way . . ." The raccoon leaned toward the cat. "You said I was messy and dangerous. I'll admit to dangerous, but I am certainly not messy!"

"Wait a minute," Puff said. "You have to admit that you make messes."

"That's different. All raccoons make messes. That's expected. But I'm not messy! I'll show you. Follow me." Eddie twisted and dropped off the woodpile.

"Where are you going?" Puff asked.

The raccoon waddled toward the long grass.

"I haven't had dinner," Puff yelled.

Fast Eddie disappeared behind a rhododendron.

I'm not going to follow him, Puff thought. *I hate it when he tells me what to do. I can do what I want.*

Mrs. Plotkin kissed Sammy good-night. "Let's say our prayers," she said.

"God bless Mom and Dad, Puff and Kitty," Sammy began.

"Are you or aren't you my best friend?" It was the raccoon's voice, but two termites thought the large green bush was talking.

Puff stretched. Her back humped and her tail straightened. She sat down, gazed across the back field, and jumped off the woodpile.

Mr. Plotkin pulled out a red file entitled, "Home Improvements." He laid it on the kitchen counter and made three notations on a yellow pad:

1. Mow Back Field
   —sharpen blades.
   (hardware store)

2. Buy New Mailbox
   Post, Cement
   (hardware store).

3. Figure Out Raccoon
   Problem.

5

PUFF REACHED Fast Eddie's hole in time to see his tail disappear. She sat down and gazed at a line of pine trees.

I don't care what it looks like down there, she thought. *It's probably full of bugs.* She rotated her shoulder backward and licked the fur above her chest. *Besides, he's never invited me down there before.*

"Hurry up!" The raccoon's voice was muffled.

Puff contemplated a clump of black-eyed Susans and fans of pale green ferns. *I bet it's dirty. It probably is.* A square of moss was placed in front of the hole like a welcome mat.

What does he want me to see? Puff wondered. *It could be nice. But how could he have a nice home when all he does is make messes?*

"This is your last chance," the raccoon yelled. A bittersweet vine draped over the hole like frosting. The cat ducked beneath it.

Cats hate to move when they can't see. Puff was surrounded by dirt and blackness. Her left whiskers hit the wall. She leaned to the right. Her claws clutched the earth beneath her.

"I hate small spaces," Puff whispered.

"Just keep moving," Fast Eddie's voice beckoned. "Don't think. You'll never get anywhere if you think. Just keep going."

The tunnel pulled Puff forward and pressed her from behind, as if it were swallowing her. The passageway dropped and swerved. It twisted around a tree root and doubled back on itself. A rock stuck out of the ceiling. Puff thought of backing up, but she crawled forward on her stomach.

There better be room to turn around at the end, she thought.

A light flickered on the walls of the tunnel. Puff crawled toward it. She climbed over a ledge and dropped down. She was in a room. It was as big as Sammy Plotkin's sandbox.

Fast Eddie sat opposite the cat. "This is my home," he said quietly.

The room was bright with the glow of lightning bugs. They drifted in circles around the ceiling.

"They're my friends," the raccoon explained.

Puff stared at the wall. There were dried wildflowers pressed into the dirt. Fast Eddie nodded toward the purple violets and buttercups. "I like this side the best," he said.

On the opposite wall, there were grasses and stalks of mint. They looked like they were growing out of the floor. The whole room smelled like iced tea.

"I like that side better," the cat said.

"No. It's not finished. It needs more herbs."

Puff's eyes moved back and forth across the floor. It was covered with sunflower seeds, each one fitted into its own space. It looked like gray-and-white striped tile.

"You'll never see another one like it," the raccoon bragged.

"It's amazing," Puff agreed.

In the corner of the room, there were large cushions made of bright green moss. In front of the cushions, there was a smooth rock with a white circle around it.

"I use that as a table," Eddie said. "It's a goodluck rock from Mrs. Plotkin's garden. She got it at the ocean and it still smells salty."

"How did you know that?" Puff asked.

"You told me," the raccoon chuckled. "You can learn a lot from listening."

There was a spark, like a flashbulb.

"What's that?" Puff asked.

"What?"

"Behind you."

"It's nothing," insisted the raccoon.

"What is it?"

"You can't see it."

"I want to." The cat crawled forward.

"All right!" The raccoon hesitated, then moved sideways. Behind him, a tangle of wires and springs rose out of a pinecone. Light sparkled off the shiny, well-cared-for surfaces.

"What is it?" the cat demanded.

"I'll tell you, but don't you ever tell anyone. Ever! Promise?" The cat nodded. "I mean it," the raccoon said. "I'll kill you if you do."

"I won't,' Puff said. "I promise."

"It plays music."

"What?"

"It plays music," Eddie yelled.

"You're kidding," Puff gasped.

"I knew you'd make fun of me," Eddie said.

"I'm not!" Puff giggled.

"Yes, you are, but I don't care. I made it with

pieces I found in the barn. I like it. My mother taught me how to sing."

"You sing?" The cat bit the corners of her mouth.

"You're going to have to go," said the raccoon.

Puff looked away. "I'm sorry," she said. "Really, I'm sorry. Seriously, are there other rooms?"

"The bedroom's not finished. I made a bed out of that purple dryer lint we found on the garage floor."

"Sounds comfortable," the cat said, but she couldn't stop smiling.

Fast Eddie's claws extended, curled, and disappeared. Suddenly, his paw was in the air. It swiped at the cat's face and pounded the wall. Puff jumped

and smashed her head on the ceiling.

"Why'd you do that?" the raccoon bellowed.

"You scared me!"

"I was trying to scare the worms." Again, the paw swung through the air and smashed the wall. "They tunnel in here and ruin my flowers. They drive me crazy. When I hear them coming, I hit the walls. It makes them change direction."

"Oh," said the cat. She shook her head. Three dead bugs fell to the floor.

"Oh no," the raccoon groaned. "Puff, you've killed three of them. Do you know how hard it is to catch lightning bugs?" he added. "Come on, you have to go. I want to clean up." He began to fidget.

"I'm leaving," said the cat. She pivoted and climbed into the tunnel.

"Remember, don't think," the raccoon yelled after her. "Just keep moving. It's always better not to think."

Puff melted into the darkness. *That was so strange,* she thought as she crawled upward. *It didn't seem real.*

The cat emerged into the light. She shook, but dirt stuck to her fur. She sat back on her hind legs. Her tail floated down beside her.

The cat looked up at the sky. It was filled with

stars. Some were just arriving and they flickered. *That's where Eddie got the idea for his ceiling,* she thought.

Puff looked at the hole. *It's just a hole. It's just like any other hole.* The cat frowned. *Maybe it was a dream. The floor and the cushions . . . and that instrument! There was a strange light.* The cat lifted her face to the sky and closed her eyes. *It was too neat. Fast Eddie couldn't be that neat. It must have been a dream.*

A dazed lightning bug lifted off the cat's head and flew awkwardly away.

6

Mrs. PLOTKIN BRUSHED her teeth and remembered the cat. "Did you put Puff out?" she asked. Blue foam appeared at the corner of her mouth.

Mr. Plotkin was setting the alarm clock. "What time do you want to get up?"

"Seven." Mrs. Plotkin spat. "Have you seen the cat?"

"Not since this morning."

Mrs. Plotkin smeared pink cream across her forehead. She spoke to her reflection in the mirror. "I wonder where she is. . . ."

Puff sprawled on the front porch. Her paws floated above her as if they were on strings. She glanced up at the Plotkins' bedroom as the light clicked off.

Puff closed her eyes, tucked her nose under her paw, and breathed out slowly. She listened to two moles babbling about birdseed. The dog across the street barked for Kitty.

I wonder what happened to Jones, Puff thought, just before she fell asleep.

At two-thirty in the morning, a flea bit the cat on her left paw. A tiny head appeared in the white fur. Puff chewed and sucked. The flea fell backward onto her tongue. The cat spat and the bug somersaulted over the edge of the porch.

Puff stretched her head back and straightened her tail. She smelled the cut grass across the street and heard a barrel tip over in the garage.

Her blue eyes opened wide. A second barrel bounced on the cement floor. The cat rolled onto her paws. She crawled down the porch steps and under the lowest branches of an azalea bush. Without hesitating, she continued out the other side and across the driveway. A sharp cat shadow followed her.

Puff leaped over the daylily bed. The blossoms bent out of the way. She circled the maple tree, ignored the station wagon, and sat down in the middle of the driveway.

A voice echoed in the garage: "Where did these ropes come from?"

Puff licked her paw until it was wet. She closed her eyes and swabbed her forehead.

"What do you bet Mr. Plotkin tied this one?" A rubber lid rolled out the garage door. It made a small circle and fell.

The damp white paw passed over the eyelids.

"Yes! Beets! There must be some coffee grounds in there, too. Beets and coffee grounds and something white." Papers and plastic crunched into each other.

Puff's licks grew longer, half the length of her front leg. She ran her paw up the back of her neck, over her head, and down to her nose. Her ear flattened and popped back. She cleaned her paw with five licks and placed it on the driveway. Her tongue felt fuzzy and dry.

"Sour cream! Look at those green islands in there. Now, where are the chicken gizzards? There are always chicken gizzards. There. Oh! What a smell!" The raccoon stepped into the moonlight. A bag of gizzards hung from his mouth.

"Don't get near me with those," Puff said.

Fast Eddie crawled to the middle of the driveway, opened the paper bag with his teeth, and piled the neck, liver, and heart on top of one another.

"There's a white cup in there, Puff. Will you get

it?" he asked. The cat didn't move. "Come on. You're not hurting anyone. And I need some tinfoil. The Plotkins will never know." The raccoon glanced over his shoulder. "Are you my best friend, or aren't you?" he asked.

Puff sighed. *I guess it's all right,* she thought. *No one will ever know.* She walked into the garage and reappeared with tinfoil hanging from her mouth. Her teeth throbbed. The raccoon hummed to himself as he passed her.

A Styrofoam cup flew over Puff's head and bounced on the driveway. Fast Eddie circled the cat and batted the cup with his paw. It landed on the chicken gizzards.

"We're getting there," the raccoon said proudly. "This is going to be one of my best creations."

Puff dropped the tinfoil. "You can finish without me," she said. "I'm going back to bed." She strolled toward the back door.

"Thanks for your help," Eddie yelled after her. "You're a friend and a half."

Puff nestled into the soft dirt under the kitchen window. She listened to the hum of the refrigerator and the tick of the clock. She felt a daddy longlegs climb over her tail. She was almost asleep when she heard a whisper:

"Collision course."

Puff squinted. Jones was standing in front of her.

"What?" the cat asked.

"It's a collision course."

"Oh." Puff closed her eyes. Jones waited. The cat scowled and opened her eyes again. "What is that supposed to mean?"

"I've been around, Puff," Jones whispered. "I've learned a lot in my travels. One thing I've learned . . . raccoons never win. Your friend is on a collision course with the Plotkins, and take my word for it, he won't win."

"Just because you go on trips," Puff said irritably, "doesn't mean you know everything."

"You'll see," Jones interrupted. He ducked under a leaf and was gone.

Puff wanted to go back to sleep, but the harder she tried, the more often she opened her eyes. She watched the sky go from black to blue and the stars dissolve. She heard the newspaper land with a SPLAT at the end of the driveway and the first burp of the automatic coffee machine.

7

"GO ON OUT," Mr. Plotkin said. Kitty's toe-nails clicked on the porch steps. The screen door slammed and leather slippers whacked along the driveway.

Puff was half asleep, but she climbed the steps to the back door. She didn't want to miss her chance to get inside for breakfast. She glanced at the tower of garbage. It looked bigger in the daylight.

Mr. Plotkin strolled toward the porch. "They lost again!" he said.

He won't notice, Puff thought. *He'll keep reading and he won't see it.*

As if the cat had spoken out loud, Mr. Plotkin glanced up from the newspaper and looked at the yellow chicken fat, the cups, the gizzards, and the wrinkled beets. The sour cream sparkled.

A noise rose up Mr. Plotkin's throat.

Puff crouched. The door swung open. The cat dashed in front of the slippers and scurried into the kitchen. When the newspapers slammed on the table, Puff left the floor. When she landed, she came down on top of her tail.

"Here's your breakfast, Puff," Mrs. Plotkin said. She filled the dish on the cellar stair landing with fresh circles of cat food.

"He got into the trash again," Mr. Plotkin announced. "It's all over the driveway."

"I know," Mrs. Plotkin said. "I heard you yell."

"Rocky?" Sammy asked.

"Yes!" Mr. Plotkin dug into the paper for the sports section.

"Didn't you rope up the barrels?" Mrs. Plotkin asked. She handed Mr. Plotkin a cup of coffee.

"Of course I did. Is there sugar in it?"

"Two teaspoons."

"Then how'd he get in, Dad?" Sammy asked.

"He undid the ropes."

Sammy grinned. "Rocky's pretty smart, don't you think?"

"I'm not going to spend one more morning cleaning garbage off the driveway," Mr. Plotkin declared. "I'm going to take care of him this weekend."

Mr. Plotkin climbed the back stairs two at a time. Sammy followed. His bare feet were silent.

Puff cut through the hall and raced up the front stairs. She stopped on the landing, pivoted, sat down, and listened.

Mr. Plotkin opened his closet door. He stared into the back. Behind the green and blue sweaters there was a long gray case. The brass zipper gleamed.

"Why are you looking at your gun?" Sammy asked. One hand was in his bathrobe pocket. His fingers surrounded a toy tank.

Mr. Plotkin whirled around. "What are you doing?" he gasped. "You surprised me!" He closed the closet door. "Don't you ever touch that shotgun, Sammy. Do you hear me?"

"Is it loaded?"

"Stay away from it!" Mr. Plotkin started down the front stairs. Puff shot by him and hid under a bed.

Sammy waited until he heard his mother ask, "What's wrong, George?" Then he opened the closet door and looked inside.

8

PUFF STARED through the bedspread fringe at the shoes in Mrs. Plotkin's closet. *What am I going to do?* she wondered. They were lined up like sparrows on a telephone wire, but Puff didn't notice. *Maybe I should talk to Jones.*

The cat's head surfaced through the fringe. She padded across the rug and bare floor to the green carpet in the hall. She heard screams and gunshots. *Sammy's watching television,* she thought. "Hi! How's he doing?" It was Mrs. Plotkin on the telephone. "How could they be in tenth place?" Mr. Plotkin's voice came from the living room. *He's in the blue chair with the sports section,* the cat decided.

Puff coasted down the stairs, keeping close to the wall. She hesitated at the library door. Sammy was staring at the square of light. "This is your last

chance," said a husky voice. Puff continued down the hall. *I'll get Mrs. Plotkin to put me out,* she thought. She stood next to the coiled telephone cord and waited.

"That's terrible," Mrs. Plotkin said. "What can I do to help? I'll make a dinner. Poor thing, the chicken pox in the summer is so awful."

Puff spotted Kitty. She was curled up on her plaid dog bed like a dinner roll. The cat wandered by the back door and sat in front of the dog's face.

"Wake up," she whispered.

Kitty's head snapped back into her shoulders. She held her breath.

"I have to go out. Nobody is paying attention. You have to bark."

"What?" Kitty said. "I was sound asleep. I'm not barking. If I do, they'll put me out." She lowered her head onto her paw and closed her eyes. "You interrupted a great dream. I was saving Sammy. I'll bark later. Go away."

"I have to go out now," the cat persisted. "Right now!"

Kitty opened one eye. "Forget it!"

Puff strolled toward the kitchen. She curved around Mrs. Plotkin's bare feet.

"What if I went to the market for you?" Mrs. Plotkin scribbled on a pad of paper.

A white paw landed in a circle of raspberry jam. Puff sat and lifted it to her mouth.

Too sweet, she thought. A seed caught in her teeth. She placed her paw on the floor and snuffed.

Tuna fish! The cat recognized her favorite smell. Her eyes drifted across the white counter. She spotted an aluminum lid pointing to the ceiling.

Puff lifted off the floor and landed next to a red pepper. Her tongue curved around the sharp edge and dipped into the can.

"Get off the counter," Mrs. Plotkin scolded.

The smooth oil coated the cat's teeth. A drop appeared below her whiskers and sank into the fur. The tongue scooped again, pulling chunks of fish into her mouth. The cat turned and jumped through Mrs. Plotkin's outstretched arms.

"Honestly, Puff, you know better." Mrs. Plotkin returned to the telephone.

"That cat is going to give us diseases," Mr. Plotkin yelled.

Puff wandered into the living room. She avoided the tall black screen and ducked under the coffee table. Her whiskers brushed the mahogany leg.

Mr. Plotkin was half submerged in the velvet chair. The open newspaper covered most of his body. The cat studied two fists and two bare legs.

"We're going to have a great team next year," Mr. Plotkin said.

Puff squeezed between a table and a couch and sat down behind a wing chair. Enormous flowers were splattered across the upholstery. They looked like they were screaming. Puff lifted her front paws and placed them on a peach daylily. The claws punched through the glazed material. The left paw moved higher, past the pink hollyhocks. The right stabbed a peony bud. Puff arched her spine, rolled her weight into her elbows, and hung from her claws. The muscles in her back stretched, relaxed, and throbbed. The white tail waved with pleasure.

Puff plucked with her claws, dragging them through the leaves and petals.

"Stupid cat!"

Puff was in the air, hanging by her neck. Her throat tightened and she opened her mouth. The dining room rug passed beneath her. Her tail brushed the corn muffins on the stove. Mr. Plotkin kicked Kitty's tin dish into the woodwork. The screen door whined.

The cat soared over the cobblestone path. Her legs spread apart. Four paws hit the driveway. The tar was cool and flat, but it felt like thumbtacks. Pain zigzagged up the cat's legs, but her face was expressionless.

The door slammed.

9

JONES PIROUETTED on the lower branches of the chestnut tree. He pretended not to notice the cat. Puff settled into the cool ivy at the base of the tree and waited for the burning to drain from her legs. She looked up at the squirrel.

Mrs. Plotkin glanced through the window in the front door. *Puff's going after a bird,* she thought. She knocked on the window and said, "You leave the birds alone." Puff watched her lips move.

"I hate to give advice," Jones said, "but I think you should steer clear of that raccoon."

The pain lingered in Puff's claws and made her disagreeable. "Fast Eddie is my friend," she said. "He may not be perfect, but he doesn't pretend to be. He doesn't care what people think. Are you perfect, Jones?"

There was a silence. Jones's voice was crisp when he answered. "I'm a lot closer."

"Would the Plotkins describe you as perfect?" the cat asked. " 'We've got red squirrels in the attic again,' they'd say. 'They've chewed through the gutters.' Mr. Plotkin is always complaining about the money he spends on the wooden gutters. And Mrs. Plotkin thinks you're going to start a fire. 'Everyone knows that red squirrels chew on wires,' she says."

"We do not!" Jones stomped his foot on the branch. A piece of bark dislodged and spun into the ivy. The squirrel hopped three steps in one direction, whirled, and hopped back. "Listen, Puff," Jones ranted. "A lot of red squirrels are born in

attics. What right have people got to take away our homes? They board up our holes every year! How would you feel?"

Puff sighed and gazed across the lawn.

"You wouldn't understand," Jones added, "because you're a cat."

"How can you criticize Fast Eddie?" Puff asked. "He may be destructive, but so are you."

"You mean you don't see a difference between returning to your place of birth and ripping up a cornfield for the fun of it?"

"Sometimes Eddie gets carried away," Puff said softly. "He just wants to outsmart the Plotkins. He says people are ruining the world."

"Well, they are," agreed the squirrel. Jones tiptoed to the end of the branch. He waited for the tree to respond. The limb sank. Leaves floated up beside his ears. The squirrel twirled and charged toward the trunk. He stopped abruptly above the cat's head.

"However, I don't see how piling rotten food on the driveway is improving things. Do you, Puff?" The cat closed her eyes. Jones's head dropped below the branch. "The point is . . . those Plotkins love their home and they're going to protect it. If you stick by your friend, you could get hurt. And what if Fast Eddie doesn't help you? What if your best friend doesn't turn out to be such a good friend after all?"

"That wouldn't happen," Puff said quickly. It made her mad that Jones was criticizing her friend when he wasn't there to defend himself. "Fast Eddie isn't like that," she insisted. A flea crawled under the cat's armpit, but Puff ignored the tickle.

"There's something you may not know, Jones," the cat said. "Fast Eddie is lucky. He always has been. He says, 'I may not be brilliant, but I am lucky. And I'll take luck over brains any day.' He'll be all right."

Jones leaped onto the trunk. He turned and raced toward the ground. A few feet above the cat, he curled right and bolted straight up. He sprang onto a telephone wire and proceeded, one foot in front of the other. Puff looked up at the squirrel's stomach. Jones glanced down. "Luck, like daylight, runs out," he said. He hurdled the electric wire. His paws hooked the end of a pine branch and he swung out of sight.

Squirrels are so dramatic, Puff thought irritably. *At least Eddie's real and he doesn't pretend to know everything.*

A Japanese beetle crossed in front of Puff's white paws. The brown wings had a purple luster. Puff had watched Mrs. Plotkin pick the insects out of blossoms and squeeze them between her fingers. "Leave my roses alone," she'd say.

Puff snorted. The beetle flew onto his back. His tiny feet scurried. *Why does he run when he knows he's not getting anywhere?* the cat wondered.

Puff stood up. Her tail rose into the air and batted at imaginary flies.

"I wish I'd never talked to Jones," Puff whispered. "He didn't help at all."

The cat wandered toward the side porch. She stopped and sniffed. *A mouse rotting under the porch.* She looked down the back field. *Two butterflies, a crow, and five chickadees,* she counted. The birds dispersed and the butterflies accompanied each other into an apple tree.

Mrs. Plotkin opened the front door. "You didn't eat your breakfast, Puff," she said. "Are you feeling all right?"

Puff wanted to tell Fast Eddie about the "collision course" and the shotgun, but she knew what he'd say. She could hear his voice as if he were sitting behind her: "Don't worry about me. I'm lucky."

The cat meandered toward the porch steps. A barn swallow dropped out of the sky, missed the white ear by inches, and soared around the house. Puff prowled up the steps and walked casually through the open door.

10

MR. PLOTKIN was halfway into the refrigerator. "Do we have any pickles?" he asked.

"I'll get them." Mrs. Plotkin plucked a jar off the door. A pickle slid beside Sammy's sandwich and another next to a mound of lettuce greens and red peppers. "You're not considering shooting Rocky, are you?" she asked.

Mr. Plotkin sat down, picked up his fork, and speared a cherry tomato. "I don't want to," he answered.

Puff squatted in front of her bowl. She lifted the dry pellets into her mouth and crunched. Sammy licked the juice off his pickle.

"First, I'm going to try and trap him," Mr. Plotkin said. Puff stopped chewing. "I'm renting a Havahart trap. It catches them alive."

"Then you shoot him?" Sammy asked.

Puff looked through the crack in the cellar door. Mrs. Plotkin's hands smoothed a red napkin across her thigh.

"No," Mr. Plotkin said. "You catch them alive, take them away, and release them. Of course, it's illegal. I'll do it at night."

"What do you mean?" Mrs. Plotkin's fork hesitated in midair. "Why is it illegal?"

"You can't capture raccoons or skunks and drop them on other people's property. It just transfers the problem. I'll take Rocky to the conservation land."

Puff took three swallows of water. Sammy made a hole in the bread with his thumb. He picked up the sandwich and bit into the hole. Tuna fish oozed between the crusts. "What if the trap doesn't work?" he mumbled.

"Don't talk with your mouth full." Mrs. Plotkin picked a lemon wedge out of her tea and chewed on it.

Sammy swallowed. "Then you shoot him?"

Puff sucked more food into her mouth. She held it on her tongue.

"Raccoons are hard to trap. It's so easy for them to get the chocolate chip ice cream out of the trash, why should they squeeze into a trap?" Mr. Plotkin cut a purple onion slice in half. The knife tapped on the china plate. "The problem is that raccoons carry diseases. We can't have them around. They could infect Puff and Kitty, not to mention us. They're very dirty animals."

Puff bit down hard. Her teeth dug into her lip. Warm blood seeped into her food. Blood and particles of dried liver sat on her tongue.

"One way or another," Mr. Plotkin said, "Rocky's got to go."

Sammy brushed crumbs off his lap.

Kitty rose from her dog bed. She slipped under the table. Her tongue fell forward and swept the floor below Sammy's dangling shoelaces.

"Go to bed," Mr. Plotkin bellowed.

Kitty gathered the last morsel, bumped Mr. Plotkin's knee, and ambled back to bed.

11

PUFF JUMPED UP into the blue velvet chair in the living room. She circled the cushion and dropped onto her side. Her chin rested on the end of her tail and her eyes closed. The muscles in her legs and up the back of her neck loosened. Her whiskers drooped.

They'll never catch him, Puff thought. *Not in a trap. Eddie will laugh at the Havahart. They'll have to shoot him. Would Mr. Plotkin shoot a raccoon? Would Mrs. Plotkin let him? Sammy would love it. If Mr. Plotkin gets mad enough, Mrs. Plotkin won't be able to stop him.*

Mrs. Plotkin smiled at Puff. She fluffed the pillows on the couch and thought, *There is nothing more peaceful than a sleeping cat.*

When would he do it? Puff wondered. *In the middle of the night? He wouldn't be able to see. At* sunset? Eddie's been coming out more and more at sunset. Would he wait by his hole? He knows where the hole is. He'd never shoot him in the garage. I wonder if he's a good shot. He shoots little doves with that gun. How could he miss a raccoon? What if Mr. Plotkin kills Fast Eddie? I have to stop it. I'll tell Eddie what Mr. Plotkin's going to do. He'll get scared. He'll go away. I can't stop Mr. Plotkin so I have to stop Eddie.

Puff heard breathing. She opened her eyes and saw Sammy's lips.

"Boo!" he screamed.

12

PUFF LEANED INTO the hole. "Anybody home?" she shouted. The words bounced back in her face. "Body home? Body home? Body home?"

"Be with you in a minute. Minute. Minute." The voice boiled up from down below.

The cat's head turned toward the sun. She looked up and shut her eyes. The warmth seeped through her eyelids and her fur.

"What's up?" Fast Eddie's head popped out of the hole. A pile of fresh dirt sat between his ears.

"You have to leave the Plotkins alone," Puff said.

"What?" The dirt slid down the back of his head.

"They're getting really angry."

"Why are they angry?" the raccoon asked.

"Because you make a mess."

Eddie leaned toward the cat. "Have you ever been to the town dump, Puff?"

The cat shook her head.

"I got lost in there once. There was trash everywhere, as far as you could see in all directions. I'm not the only one who makes a mess!"

"But you're the one who's going to get trapped," Puff whispered.

"Trapped!" The raccoon grinned. "Let them try."

"Jones says you're on a collision course with the Plotkins. He thinks your luck is going to run out . . . like daylight."

Eddie scowled. "Puff! You're listening to a red squirrel? They can predict the weather, because that's all they ever think about, but they don't know anything about raccoons. I hate the way they're always warning and advising. Besides, are the Plotkins smarter than I am? Look at all the stupid things they've done. They can't even tie decent knots. How could I possibly end up in a Plotkin trap?"

"I don't know," Puff said. She stared at the ground. Two red ants struggled over a blade of grass. They teetered on the peak and somersaulted into the sunlight. Their bodies turned the color of a new penny.

"I appreciate your concern," Eddie said. "It's nice to have friends who worry about you. However, it's the Plotkins you should worry about."

"Why?"

"Because there's a full moon tomorrow night."

"Oh no," Puff gasped.

"If you want to have a little fun, be here. Midnight. Tomorrow." Fast Eddie backed down the hole. He disappeared, like water going down a drain. The ants stared at the cat.

Puff picked her way back through the field. The wildflowers bobbed and gyrated as she stepped on their stems.

Sammy Plotkin stared out the bathroom window. "Why are the flowers dancing?" he asked.

Mrs. Plotkin smiled and continued washing out the bathtub.

Puff sat down on the lawn. Her tail twitched. *I forgot to tell him about the gun,* she thought.

Mr. Plotkin sat erect on the tractor seat as though he were roosting. He bounced toward the last rectangle of uncut grass. The green blades submitted, losing their heads between the doughnut-shaped tires. The tractor purred.

Mr. Plotkin stepped on the brake and surveyed the lawn. He admired the highways of cut grass.

As parallel as lines on a page, he thought. He checked the patch of newly seeded lawn. *It's coming up perfectly. All the seeding, fertilizing, rolling, and watering has been worth it.*

The tractor grumbled into first and idled into the

garage. Mr. Plotkin emerged, brushing vigorously. He swept the grass off the driveway, bent over, and picked a gum wrapper out of the pile. He turned and carried the broom to the back steps.

Puff circled the oak tree and slumped onto the warm tar. A gray titmouse alighted on a branch above her, hesitated, and pushed off. Bicycles passed the end of the driveway.

"Slow down," someone yelled.

Another voice screamed, "Hurry up!"

Puff's tail lifted off the driveway and curled above her. *A full moon!* she thought.

Sammy placed his black police car on the driveway. The antenna wobbled. He breathed out slowly.

Puff watched the shadows play across her fur. She smelled steak bones in the trash. *What's Eddie planning?* she wondered.

Two spiders who were crawling up the downspout hesitated. They watched the cat close her eyes and roll her head back. A patch of sun fell on the fur under her chin.

"She's putting on weight," gossiped one of the spiders.

"I don't know how," said the other. "She hasn't caught a mouse in weeks!"

The car started forward. Sammy crushed the blue

and red buttons on the controller. The car accelerated. Headlights flashed.

"I'm putting up the new mailbox," Mr. Plotkin yelled. "I need some help."

The tires spun and the car shot across the driveway. Puff opened her eyes. She noticed an odd light on her stomach and glanced sideways. She arched her back and levitated. The black form flew beneath her. The antenna slapped her in the eye. The police car rocketed off the tar and disappeared into the grass clippings. Puff landed on her paws. The antenna bobbed.

"Wow!" Sammy whooped.

Puff bolted into the garage. She jumped up on the tractor seat. It was still warm from Mr. Plotkin's bottom. She blinked and gasped for air.

"Are you all right, Puff?" Mrs. Plotkin stood in the garage door. A hand glided down the cat's back. "Let's go inside," she said. She lifted the cat and cuddled her against her chest.

"I just wanted to see how fast my car could go," Sammy whined.

Puff's head twisted over Mrs. Plotkin's elbow. *Liar,* she thought.

"You didn't aim at her?" Mrs Plotkin asked.

"No!" Sammy started to cry. A large tear rolled toward his lips.

Puff arched her back and dropped out of Mrs. Plotkin's arms. *I'm not going to listen to this,* she thought as she landed. *He tried to kill me.*

"Why's Sammy crying?" Mr. Plotkin asked.

"He tried to hit Puff with his police car," Mrs. Plotkin replied. "He's been bothering her all day."

"No, I haven't!" Sammy screamed.

Mr. Plotkin smiled. "It's not a good idea to use Puff as a target," he said. "Come on, Sammy, let's dig a hole for the new mailbox."

"I finished stenciling it," Mrs. Plotkin said

proudly. "It's all ready to go. It says PLOTKIN in huge letters. They fit perfectly."

"Great! First, we dig a hole, Sam."

"I'm going to touch up the back door," Mrs. Plotkin interrupted, "so don't come in this way, or you'll get black paint on you."

"All right. Then we mix cement and pour it in the hole."

"He won't last long," Mrs. Plotkin advised.

"The post goes in next. Let's get the wheelbarrow."

Mrs. Plotkin headed for the barn. "When he gets tired, send him into the kitchen. I'm going to make brownies."

Puff shook her head in irritation and crawled into the flower garden. She sat next to a purple cosmos. As she licked her left paw, she thought about how much she disliked Sammy Plotkin. Her stomach growled and she remembered that she had eaten only a bite of breakfast and two bites of lunch.

"I'm not going in the back door," she decided, "and risk getting paint on my tail again. It took forever for the hair to grow back last time. I'll take the tunnel."

"Isn't Puff brilliant?" Mrs. Plotkin had exclaimed the first time the cat had used the tunnel. She'd picked cobwebs out of Puff's whiskers.

"How'd she get in?" Sammy had asked.

"I guess she found a tunnel. When we moved in, this house was filled with squirrels. I thought they came through the gutters, but there must be a tunnel in the cellar."

"Why'd they come in?"

"Someone stored birdseed in the cellar. Squirrels love birdseed more than anything," Mrs. Plotkin had answered.

"How'd the squirrels know about the birdseed?"

"Squirrels know those things."

Puff stepped onto a path of stones. They gave way under her paws. She followed the stones along the clapboards to the corner of the barn. A fat fly flew into a window above her and fell backward into a web.

"Let's move Puff's food to the top of the cellar stairs," Mrs. Plotkin had said. "That way Kitty won't be able to eat it."

Puff thought it was a wonderful idea. She hated eating next to the dog. Kitty's gulping and spitting revolted her. The dog ate fast and then swung her mouth into the cat's dish.

"Sorry," she'd say. "I get confused. It all looks the same."

Puff squatted and squeezed through a hole in the foundation. Her back legs shot pebbles onto the lawn.

The barn was black except for three narrow triangles of light. The stall doors, an old mattress, and a crib loomed in front of the cat. Puff proceeded around the paint cans. She crossed in front of the rakes and behind a bag of peat moss. In a dark corner of the barn, the cement floor had disintegrated. Puff stepped into the hole.

The crawl space under the playroom was filled with enormous heating ducts wrapped in blue plastic. The cat moved quickly beneath them. She stepped over a red-and-white soda can and avoided a pile of cigarette butts. The clinking of a zipper in the dryer distracted her. She didn't hear the rustling.

There was a circle of light in the foundation wall. It stared straight ahead like an eye. Puff sprang at the light and landed on the cellar floor. She was on her way to the stairs when she stopped.

Digging and snarling, spitting and moaning echoed in the tunnel. Then it was quiet. A nose and a face appeared in the black circle.

Fast Eddie spat onto the cellar floor. He cleared his sinuses and spat again. "I got insulation up my nose," he complained.

Someone had left the cellar light on. The glare made everything sharp and real, especially Eddie's face. The cat would have hissed, but she was stunned. It had never occurred to her that the raccoon would enter the house.

Puff was as still as Mrs. Plotkin's glass paperweight.

The raccoon snuffed and spat.

13

"CAN WE MAKE the brownies now?" Sammy asked.

Mrs. Plotkin placed the cover on the can of black paint and held the door open.

"I don't like putting up a mailbox," Sammy said. "Can I lick the bowl?"

Chocolate squares and a stick of butter tumbled into the dish and disappeared in the microwave.

"Cat got your tongue?" the raccoon asked. He squeezed out of the tunnel and dropped onto the cellar floor.

Sammy climbed up into a chair. He broke two eggs into a yellow plastic bowl and threw the shells over his shoulder into the sink. Mrs. Plotkin handed him a whisk.

"You do it, Mom," Sammy said.

The raccoon inspected the cellar. His eyes scanned the jars of homemade pink jellies and the shelf of Sammy's outgrown boots.

"Where's the food?" he asked.

"The food?" Puff gasped. "You're going to steal my food?"

"They'll give you more," Eddie said. "I promise. You won't even miss a meal." He shook dirt off his right paw. "Besides, I adore cat food."

The microwave beeped. Chocolate and butter swirled with the eggs and sugar.

"Can I have a lick?" Sammy asked as he stared into the bowl.

"I can't believe I told you about the tunnel," Puff whispered, "and my food on the cellar stairs. I'll never tell you anything ever again."

Eddie started toward the stairs. "You're being ridiculous," he said.

"It was a secret," Puff yelled.

"I didn't tell anyone," Eddie yelled back.

The oven door opened and the pan skidded onto the rack. Sammy licked the back of his hand. Black batter covered his chin.

"We're going to get into trouble!"

"I can handle the Plotkins."

Puff began to shiver. "I don't believe you're doing this. My best friend!"

"No one's going to let you starve," Eddie insisted. "There's always more for you. But who takes care of me? Besides, aren't best friends supposed to share? You're just thinking about yourself." Fast Eddie rose up on his hind legs and twisted toward the cat.

"Come on," he said, "I'm a raccoon. Raccoons have stolen food for thousands of years, long before there were Plotkins on this earth. If we didn't, that would be the end of us. Anyway, I was here before the Plotkins. I liked the other owners better. They weren't so fussy." He dropped onto his front paws, hesitated, and looked back over his shoulder.

"Do I try to change you, Puff?" he asked. "Do I tell you it's disgusting the way you depend on people? You're no more independent than Sammy Plotkin. But you're a cat. I know that. Take the free food, but remember—everyone isn't so lucky."

Mrs. Plotkin walked over to the sink and turned on the water. A fork fell down the disposal. Sammy lifted his shirt and licked a teardrop of batter off the front.

Eddie climbed the stairs effortlessly. His head fell into the cat's bowl. Puff sat back on her hind legs.

Cat food dribbled down the stairs and bounced on the cement floor. Puff's bowl glided through the air like a Frisbee. It bounced off the shelf of jellies and landed on the floor. The jars wobbled.

The water ceased. "What was that?" Mrs. Plotkin asked. She dropped an orange sponge on the counter.

Fast Eddie grunted. Mrs. Plotkin's sneakers squeaked. The door opened. Daylight filled the stairwell. Puff couldn't move.

A green barrel rolled sideways down the cellar stairs. Brown kernels of dog food exploded like pop-

corn. Mrs. Plotkin screamed. The door slammed.

Fast Eddie took his time coming down the stairs. When he reached the tunnel, he swung around.

"You're my best friend, Puff," he announced. "Including all raccoons."

An hour later, Mr. Plotkin nailed boards across the hole in the cellar wall. Puff watched from behind the freezer. The cat dish was moved back to its original position, next to Kitty's.

Puff took a nap on Sammy's bed. She watched birds fly by the window and listened to mice in the

walls. She decided that she didn't care about the full moon, but mostly she didn't care about Fast Eddie.

The next morning, Puff took a shortcut. She strolled through the barn in connecting half circles, by the horse stall and around the barrel of soft drink cans. She didn't see the raccoon.

"People are so smart, aren't they, Puff?" Fast Eddie was sitting on a mattress picking fleas out of his armpit. The cat cowered. Eddie look up and smiled. "Come over here," he said. "I have to tell you what happened." Eddie pulled a flea off his stomach and dropped it onto his tongue.

The cat jumped up on a pile of newspapers. She stared at the bright colors of the comics that surrounded her paws. The drawings of cats and dogs leaping into the air annoyed her.

"Did you know they cleaned up the whole cellar? I don't know why they bothered. I thought the mess looked great. Of course, those Plotkins are so tidy!" Eddie dug into his right ear. "Aren't you wondering what the Plotkins did with all that food?"

Puff didn't answer.

The raccoon held his paw up in the air. "Want a flea?" Puff shook her head.

"Still mad at me, eh? Come on. Take a flea. Consider it a peace offering."

Puff crouched. "I don't need a best friend," she

said without looking up. "I have the Plotkins. They make me feel warm and safe."

"That's true," agreed the raccoon.

Puff looked up at Fast Eddie. He was slouched on top of the mattress, combing through the fur under his chin with his claws. His left foot tapped against the wall. "Not another one," Eddie groaned. He gritted his teeth and yelled, "Got him." He grinned at the cat.

"If that's what you want," Eddie said, "to be warm and safe, then stay away from me. I'd find it a little dull. All that napping and chewing and not much else. And you're so dependent. Doesn't it make you mad when you meow for dinner and they say, 'Quiet! I'll feed you in a minute'?"

Puff didn't answer. Eddie knew it made her mad, because she'd complained about it.

"The Plotkins would drive me crazy," the raccoon said. "I don't know how you put up with them. I saw Sammy try to kill you with that car. I was really worried. I don't think Mr. Plotkin was too worried, though. All he worries about is peeling paint." The raccoon stretched toward the ceiling. "The cellar. Aren't you curious what happened?"

Of course, the cat was curious.

"The food. Where do you think it went? Come on. Guess."

"I don't care."

"Well, think about it. You know the Plotkins. What would they do with it?"

"Throw it out."

"Bingo!" Eddie's eyes twinkled like Christmas lights. "Those clever Plotkins put all that food in the trash."

Puff realized why Eddie looked so pleased. Generations of raccoons had faced trash barrels. They'd worked on their techniques until they were perfect. The secrets had been passed down.

"Getting into a barrel," Eddie often said, "is as easy as falling asleep."

"I'm going to get fat," the raccoon grumbled. "I've even brought some of the food home. I'm storing it under my bed. I hope I don't get sick of it." Eddie crawled to the end of the mattress. He shook his head. "What would I ever do without you?" he asked.

Mr. Plotkin lifted a box out of the back of the station wagon. Sunlight slid across the trapdoors and danced along the steel wires. He carried it around the back of the barn and placed it on the lawn next to the patio. *This better work,* he thought.

Mrs. Plotkin watched from the dining room window. "It'll never work," she said to Sammy.

14

IT WAS A clear night, unusually cool for late August. The full moon rested on top of the trees like a cherry on a hot fudge sundae. A jet drew a line across the sky. Far below, two sparrows flapped home.

Sammy rolled onto his stuffed dinosaur. He drooled and pulled the animal closer.

Mr. Plotkin hung his bathrobe on the hook in his closet. He glanced up at the leather case.

"Do you think the trap will work?" Mrs. Plotkin asked as she kicked her slippers under the bed.

"Maybe." Mr. Plotkin shut the closet door. "I hope so. For Rocky's sake."

Puff lay on the woodpile, listening to crickets. She curled her left paw and extended her right. Her head slumped onto the fur above her elbow. Her tail felt stiff and heavy. She kept hearing the words "collision course." Puff considered spending the night on the old sofa in the barn. She wished she wasn't curious. She smelled honeysuckle.

Maybe nothing will go wrong, she thought.

Jones climbed the chestnut tree and leaped into the gutter. He tiptoed forward until his paw hit a soft spot. He backed up and squatted. His teeth dug into the rotten wood.

Fast Eddie appeared at the edge of the field. He started across the lawn. The cat looked up.

He should be sleek like a criminal or Sammy's stupid police car, she thought, *but he bubbles like an inchworm.* The raccoon scrunched into the shadow of the woodpile.

"What a night!" The voice came out of the darkness. "Have you ever seen a brighter moon?"

Puff didn't answer. "You know your white fur glistens in this light, Puff," the raccoon continued. "Your whiskers even sparkle. You look magnificent. Actually, the whole world looks magnificent."

Puff wanted to tell Eddie to go home. She imagined him lying on the moss pillows with the glow of the lightning bugs drifting over him.

"What's wrong?" the raccoon asked. "Nervous? Take a deep breath."

The lawn was as white as milk. Sharp black shadows looked more real than the house and trees. Sammy's swing floated back and forth under the jungle gym.

Kitty stood up, circled her dog bed, and lay down again.

Fast Eddie stepped into the moonlight.

"Go home," the cat blurted.

"Not a chance," the raccoon answered. He started across the lawn. He headed straight for the newly seeded patch of grass.

Fast Eddie jumped into the air and came down with his paws spread apart. Mud oozed through his claws and splattered like chocolate pudding. He circled the lawn, squishing and swaying. Only a small oval in the center remained untouched.

The raccoon curled to the right and started toward the terrace. Puff closed her eyes. *He's heading for the furniture,* she thought.

"Oh, George," Mrs. Plotkin had said when the new cushions arrived, "they're as white as my cultured pearls."

When Puff opened her eyes, Eddie was on the glass coffee table. He stepped onto the sofa and smeared his paws on the back cushions. He jumped down, wandered back to the mud, and took a wide swing around the edge. He then returned to the furniture and crawled up into each chair. When he was finished, he crossed the lawn to the woodpile.

"You were right, Puff! Those Plotkins put a trap on the terrace. It has cheese in it! Can you believe it? They think I'm a mouse!" Mud dripped down the raccoon's legs. "You know, Puff," he added, "you should have joined me out there. It was really fun."

"Can't you stop now?" Puff asked.

The raccoon scowled. "Your problem is," he said, "you don't know how to have a good time. And you don't see that the Plotkins deserve this. They cut down our trees and mow our fields. There's no place to hide anymore. Remember how dizzy you were when they sprayed chemicals on the lawn? You were sick for days."

The cat looked away.

"If you want to crawl into a hole and ignore what's going on," Fast Eddie said, "fine. But I don't."

The row of pine trees down the side of the field was motionless. Puff could see faces in the branches. Some were laughing.

Kitty lay on her side. Her feet started to move and a muffled "woof" came out of her mouth. She dreamed she was chasing an animal. It was an odd mixture of a cat, a woodchuck, a rabbit, and a raccoon. The feet galloped. Suddenly, the animal turned and faced her. The dog barked out loud, waking herself up. She barked again to make herself feel better.

"Why is she barking?" Mrs. Plotkin mumbled.

"I don't know," Mr. Plotkin said. "I haven't been to sleep, anyway. Every time there's a full moon, I can't sleep. Maybe I'll get up and read."

15

FAST EDDIE TIPTOED around the woodpile. He swerved right across the driveway and passed through the garage doors. His striped tail faded into the blackness.

SCREECH! CRASH! A trash barrel fell on its side.

Puff flinched.

EEEEEEEK! BANG!

"What's he doing?" Jones whispered. His head appeared in the gutter above the cat.

"He's tipping over the trash barrels," Puff answered.

"Oh." Jones leaned forward. "I hate to admit it," the squirrel said, "but it is sort of exciting."

SMOOSH! DRAAAAAAG! CLINK!

"He broke a glass," Puff mumbled. "Jones, I can't stop him. What am I going to do?"

"Stay out of the way," Jones said. His head ducked into the gutter.

Fast Eddie emerged, dragging a pizza box with his mouth. He dropped it on the driveway. "I hate crusts," he said, as he lifted his paw. "Why do I eat them?" A pale pink tongue cleaned between the claws. "Did you hear that glass? I almost cut myself."

"Let's go home, Eddie," Puff said. "You've had a good meal."

The raccoon looked surprised. "I wouldn't call pizza crusts a good meal!"

"You could eat nuts and bugs like the rest of us," Jones said. His head reappeared.

"Do you have any idea how many nuts and bugs I'd have to eat?" the raccoon asked. "I remember you. You're Jones. Right? Puff's friend."

The squirrel nodded.

Mr. Plotkin got out of bed. He walked to his closet, opened the door, and turned on the light. He reached up and pulled down the leather case.

"Let's go home," Puff repeated. "I'm so tired."

"But you haven't seen my masterpiece!" Eddie grinned.

"What are you doing?" Mrs. Plotkin grumbled. "I'm cleaning my gun. Go back to sleep."

If Puff could have had one wish, she would have wished that Sammy would kick off his covers and scream. The windows of the Plotkin house would blaze. Fast Eddie would scurry for his hole and she would hide behind the mattress in the barn.

Puff wanted it to be over. She didn't want a masterpiece.

16

A CAR PASSED the end of the driveway. Light filled the road and splashed across trees and stone walls. A gurgling followed the light. Then the car was gone, around the corner, forgotten except for the smell of exhaust.

Kitty opened one eye. She watched the raccoon pass by the back door.

"It would be one thing if they still planted corn, but they don't even do that," Fast Eddie mumbled. He passed the bed of daylilies with the blossoms closed and sound asleep. "Who needs a field of wildflowers? It's just not the same."

"Don't follow him." Jones leaned over the gutter and yelled at the cat. "Think for yourself! You're just following Fast Eddie through life."

The raccoon reached the end of the driveway and

continued into the road. He sat down on the yellow line.

Puff started running. A bat dropped out from behind a shutter. His wings vibrated. He dipped toward the cat, changed direction, and fluttered into the night.

Puff raced by the back door. She looked like she was being chased by her shadow. It was Eddie's voice she heard: "Just keep moving, don't think." Kitty lifted her head off her paws and stared.

Jones ran diagonally up the barn roof and sprinted down the other side. He vaulted the gutter to the magnolia tree. The leaves whished. Jones continued across the tree as if the branches were as straight as a highway. Seconds later, he climbed the roof of the Plotkin house. At the chimney, he paused. He looked down at the large animal interrupting the solid line.

"Eddie!" Puff screamed. "Get out of the road!" She pulled up at the end of the driveway.

"Listen." The raccoon cocked his head.

Puff heard crickets and Jones crawling along a branch and her own heart pounding.

"See?" said Fast Eddie. "You can hear a car. It's

not as easy to hear a bicycle, but you can always hear a car. And anyone can see a car coming at night. This is really very safe."

"How come you see so many dead raccoons in the road, then?" yelled Jones.

"Please, Eddie," Puff begged. "Please come out of the road."

"You have to face your fears," Eddie said. "Face them and they'll disappear."

Puff thought she heard a mosquito. The noise was far away. Then it was on top of them. A blue haze filled the road. The raccoon stared at the light.

"Look out!" Puff squeezed her eyes shut.

"Oh no!" Jones gasped. He fainted and tumbled out of the tree.

The tires squealed. Laughing voices and rock music invaded the quiet. The tires screeched again and the car vanished around the corner.

Jones landed in Mrs. Plotkin's window box, snapping the pink geranium in the center.

Puff tried to breathe, but she couldn't. Her thoughts were far away, sitting in a tree somewhere. Warm air tickled her whiskers.

"And you thought only cats had nine lives?" the raccoon whispered.

Puff opened her eyes. Eddie's face was in front of her. His smile was so large that his mask was just a thin outline around his eyes. "Isn't this exciting?" He beamed at the cat.

"I hate your stupid games," Puff yelled. "It's all just a game to you. I don't know why I'm even here!"

"You're here because you're my best friend. And we're a great team."

"I don't want to be your best friend," the cat screamed.

The raccoon didn't seem to hear. "Remember the time Mrs. Plotkin forgot to let you in?" he said.

"During the snowstorm? We cuddled together all night long. And the time Sammy forgot to feed you two days in a row. . . . Remember? It was lucky I could get into the trash and find those chicken livers." Eddie looked up at the moon and whispered. "People will always let you down."

Mr. Plotkin climbed back into bed. He rolled over, rolled back, and stared at the window shade.

17

"HAVE YOU NOTICED the new mailbox?" Fast Eddie asked.

"What?"

"The mailbox."

"No."

"Go out in the road and look at it."

"I will not." Puff wandered off the driveway and sat on the grass. Her right hind leg lifted and pointed forward. She licked the top of it.

"Okay. Then I'll describe it. It's bright red and it's as shiny as plastic wrap. Remember the old one? It was dented and you could see the metal underneath."

The subject of the mailbox bored the cat. The Plotkins, Puff felt, were too concerned with the well-being of their mailbox.

"You're not going to believe it!" Mr. Plotkin com-

plained regularly. "The mailbox is down again! I'm so
fed up with those teenagers and their baseball bats!"

"We'll fix it," Mrs. Plotkin always said.

"Puff, are you listening to me?" Fast Eddie asked.
"What did I say?"

"I don't know," the cat answered.

"I said . . ." Fast Eddie spoke slowly, emphasizing
each word. "The mailbox will be my masterpiece."
He turned and shuffled across the lawn.

"I'll paint it red." Puff could hear Mrs. Plotkin's
voice. "And I'll stencil PLOTKIN in white letters on
both sides."

Eddie paused in front of an old maple tree. He
looked like a brown bush. His eyes moved up the
trunk of the tree. His tail swirled behind him.

Why does it have to be the mailbox? Puff wondered.

Eddie reached up with his right paw. The claws
hooked into the rough bark. He reached higher with
his left, stretching from the ground. As the raccoon
pulled himself up, he grunted. The crickets stopped
chirping.

Eddie moved toward the moon. He positioned
each paw with care and rose above it. He crawled
into the crotch of the tree, glanced down at Puff, and
continued upward.

The branches stretched out, overlapped and tangled with the leaves. The bark was as black as a new tar driveway.

"Can you see me, Puff? I don't know if you can tell from there," Eddie continued, "but this branch is rotten."

Puff squinted. She could see the branch. It twisted away from the trunk, dipped into an elbow, and reached out over the road. The end was jagged, as if it had been ripped off in a storm.

"Why are you on a rotten branch?" Puff yelled.

"Look below me," Eddie answered.

The cat's eyes dropped like a stone. Directly below Fast Eddie was the mailbox.

The cat read the letters. "P - L - O - T - K - I - N." Then she heard chewing. "N - I - K - T - O - L - P." The limb groaned. It was as if Puff thought that by reading the letters, she could make them stay there.

"Timber," Fast Eddie screamed.

The air was filled with a gruesome, splintering noise. The branch tore away from the tree. It fell cleanly through the lower limbs. When the dead wood hit the mailbox, it cut through it as if it were made of cake. The branch, mailbox, and post fell forward in slow motion and crashed onto the road.

Puff's stomach rose up into her throat.

"Ya-hoo," the raccoon hollered.

The cat stared at the mailbox. The L - O - T - K - I were shriveled and knotted, like old fruit in the trash. Only the P and the N survived.

"My masterpiece!" the raccoon sang.

The words echoed. "Masterpiece. Masterpiece."

18

A LIGHT WENT on in the house. The voices, frantic like boiling water, came through the screens on the bedroom windows. There was another light and another, until the Plotkin house glowed.

The back door burst open. Slippers smacked on the driveway.

"Stay in the house, Sammy." It was Mr. Plotkin's voice. He tied up his bathrobe as he ran. Mrs. Plotkin was right behind him, wrapped in an overcoat.

Mr. and Mrs. Plotkin stopped at the end of the driveway. They stood there as still as Sammy's toy soldiers.

"Oh no," said Mrs. Plotkin.

Puff was sure the Plotkins were staring at her. Her tongue stuck to the roof of her mouth.

"Get a flashlight." It was Mr. Plotkin. Mrs. Plotkin ran back down the driveway.

Puff jumped over the stone wall into dry leaves.

"What was that?" Mr. Plotkin yelled. He grabbed a branch from the road and threw it toward the stone wall. It was a good throw. It hit the wall and shattered. A large piece hit the cat in the head.

Puff's mind went blank. The pain spread into her ears. She couldn't see anything.

"Can I see? What happened? Why can't I come?" Sammy cried. Kitty barked twice.

"Quiet," Mr. Plotkin shrieked. The barking ceased.

"Come on, Mom! Why can't I see?"

Mrs. Plotkin followed a circle of light down the driveway. The spot moved out to the yellow line, swung left, and settled on the red mailbox.

The knotted letters and the mangled box were hideous and silent. The branch had shattered into sharp pieces of wood, pointing in all directions.

The light went straight up. It found the end of the broken limb.

"It looks like a mouth," Mrs. Plotkin said. She stared at the crooked teeth and stringy tongue reaching toward her. "I don't understand," she went on, "there's no wind."

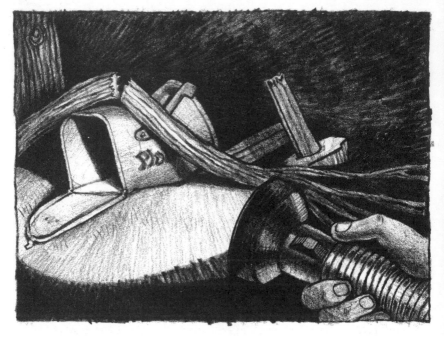

"Look again," said Mr. Plotkin.

"What?"

"See the eyes?"

"Eyes?"

"It's Rocky."

Fast Eddie leaned into the light.

"We should get the mailbox out of the road," said Mrs. Plotkin. Mr. Plotkin didn't answer. "There's nothing we can do about Rocky," she added. "He's just a raccoon."

"That's right," Mr. Plotkin said, but he didn't sound like he was agreeing. "He's just a raccoon, and I'm just human. Everyone has an excuse."

Mrs. Plotkin placed the flashlight on the grass, pointing toward the mailbox. She walked into the road, bent over, and touched the letters gently. The light illuminated her hands, her slippers, and the metal carcass. Puff watched as a second pair of hands dipped into the light. The hands and slippers disappeared and reappeared, again and again until the pieces of metal and wood were gone. Only a few chunks of bark remained.

"I'm sorry," said Mrs. Plotkin.

"I spent an entire Saturday on that mailbox."

"Yes."

Mr. Plotkin picked up the flashlight. There was a click and the light vanished. He turned and walked back down the driveway.

Mrs. Plotkin looked up into the tree. "I think you'd better find another home, Rocky," she said quietly.

"Are you coming?" Mr. Plotkin yelled from the back door. "For heaven's sakes, let's go to bed! Come on, Sammy! Go to bed!"

"What happened, Dad? What happened?" The door shut behind Mrs. Plotkin.

A few minutes later, the lights went off in the Plotkin house. They disappeared one by one, like stars before morning.

19

THE RACCOON DESCENDED the tree. He looked like a drip coming down a windowpane, slow, then fast, then slow again. He came down tail first, twisting just above the ground and dropping onto four paws. He paused and listened.

"Puff," Eddie yelled. His head swung from side to side.

There was no answer.

"Puff!" the raccoon repeated. "It's all right. They've gone to bed. Where are you?"

"Whooooooooooo." It was the sad cry of an owl.

"Probably went inside," the raccoon said. He crawled toward the driveway. "Funny," he muttered, "I thought Puff was a better friend than that. What if I'd needed help coming down the tree? I thought I could count on her."

A word throbbed in the cat's head: masterpiece, masterpiece, masterpiece. She opened her mouth, but there was no sound. *At least it's over,* she thought. Blood trickled into her eye and she blinked. The wound felt hot and tight.

Eddie ambled down the driveway. When he reached the back door, he rose up on his hind legs. Kitty's head lifted off the dog mat and she stared at the shape on the tar. She considered going back to sleep. However, she jumped to her feet, raced to the back door, and barked furiously.

The raccoon dropped onto his front legs and sprinted toward the back field. He took a wide turn around the corner of the garage. Kitty returned to bed, circled, and lay down.

Jones opened his eyes and stared up at the gutter. The geranium stalk had punctured his fur. Every time he breathed, a pain gripped his ribs. His eyes moved from star to star. He took a deep breath, grimaced, and rolled onto his side. Jones was so exhausted by the effort, he went to sleep.

20

THE NEXT MORNING Mrs. Plotkin opened the screen door for the cat. Puff wandered by her bare feet and sat down in the middle of the entryway.

"Hi, Puff," Mrs. Plotkin said without looking at the cat. She marched into the kitchen.

Puff glanced at Kitty. Her head was buried in her bowl. She looked up, scowled, and continued eating. Puff rubbed up against the door frame and stepped into the kitchen.

Mr. Plotkin was seated at the table. He held a coffee cup to his lips. Steam rose in front of his face, clouding his glasses. The newspapers sat on the table, unopened.

Mrs. Plotkin poked at bacon with a fork. It sizzled and spat.

Puff jumped into a chair. She felt like there were

metal balls banging inside her head. Sammy was sitting in the next chair, crunching inner tubes of cold cereal. Milk dripped from his lip and landed on his pajamas. He glanced at the cat.

"What happened to Puff?" Sammy mumbled.

"What's wrong?" Mrs. Plotkin asked.

"She's got a cut on her head."

"Probably got into a cat fight," Mr. Plotkin said. "She'll be all right."

Mrs. Plotkin's fingers touched the top of Puff's head. "You have quite a cut, Puff," she said.

"Does she need stitches?" Sammy asked.

"I think she'll be fine," Mrs. Plotkin replied.

"Keep Sammy inside," Mr. Plotkin said suddenly. The coffee cup rattled in the saucer.

"Why?" Sammy wanted to know.

Mrs. Plotkin stood up straight. "Let's have some bacon." She walked over to the stove, picked up the fork, and lifted a limp strip into the air.

"I have no choice," Mr. Plotkin said.

The bacon dropped on the paper towel.

"You know how I feel about guns!" Mrs. Plotkin blurted. "Sammy's exposed to too much violence as it is."

"So am I," said Mr. Plotkin. The chair screeched. Mr. Plotkin stood up. "What am I supposed to do?"

he said. "We can keep up with the dandelions, the peeling paint, and the leaks, but we're losing to the raccoons, the red squirrels, and the teenagers. I know they don't realize how much damage they do, but I am so tired of replacing everything."

"You're supposed to be a civilized human being," Mrs. Plotkin said.

"Something's burning," Sammy said.

"Oh no," Mrs. Plotkin moaned. She snapped off the burner. "Well, we have one piece of bacon," she announced.

"Give it to Sammy." Mr. Plotkin walked out of the kitchen.

Puff stared at the floor in front of the stove. She wanted to lick up the bacon grease before Kitty found it. She had heard Mr. Plotkin, but his words didn't make sense to her. She was too tired and her head hurt.

Kitty wandered into the kitchen. Her nose led her to the grease and her tongue sponged the floor. Her tail wagged.

Mr. Plotkin climbed the front stairs. His boots had a strong even beat, like a drumroll.

Sammy yelled from the kitchen, "What are you going to do, Dad? Are you going to get your gun? Are you going to kill Rocky, Dad?"

Puff gasped and jumped off her chair. She crouched under the kitchen table. Pain pressed against the back of her eyeballs. A fly landed next to her paw, but Puff didn't notice.

The boots descended the stairs.

"He's just a raccoon," Mrs. Plotkin pleaded.

"Do you have any idea how much money I spent on that mailbox?" Mr. Plotkin asked. "A hundred and one dollars and nineteen cents. And that doesn't include my time." He walked over to the kitchen table.

Puff stared at the long black barrel. It descended from Mr. Plotkin's waist like a third leg.

"Can I come?" Sammy asked.

"No!" Mr. Plotkin bellowed. He walked to the back door. Kitty sat expectantly, shifting from paw to paw. "Stay," Mr. Plotkin said. Kitty's shoulders fell and her head dropped forward.

The back door closed slowly.

Puff started to choke. She felt like something was caught in her throat. Sammy's head appeared under the table.

"Puff's throwing up," he said.

"Quickly, put her out," said Mrs. Plotkin.

Sammy squatted, grabbed the cat by the rib cage, and squeezed his hands together. When he stood up, he knocked her head into the corner of the table.

"Got her," Sammy said.

Mrs. Plotkin held the back door open. Sammy dropped Puff on the back steps. She came down hard, like mashed potatoes. The screen door brushed her tail.

Puff couldn't remember why she was on the back porch. She felt like she'd gotten very small. She was sitting in Sammy's wooden boat in the middle of a bathtub. She could hear the water. The boat was swamping. She wanted to move, but she didn't dare. She didn't know what to do.

21

MR. PLOTKIN STOPPED in the garage for a shovel. He swung it over his shoulder. He took long strides across the lawn and waded into the tall grass. The barrel of the shotgun brushed the heads of the black-eyed Susans.

Fast Eddie was curled up on his bed of purple dryer lint. He smiled as he dreamed of lobster shells. His perfect tail lifted up and floated down.

Sammy ran to the dining room window.
"Go to your room, Sammy," Mrs. Plotkin said.
"Why?" Sammy asked.
"Do as I say."

Sammy ran through the living room, knocking the blue velvet chair into the wall. He ran up the stairs and tiptoed into the bathroom. He watched his father lay the gun down and start digging.

Mrs. Plotkin took Sammy's place at the window.

Fast Eddie opened his eyes.

Puff stared at the lawn. Swells of grass floated up around the trees. The driveway looked like a black serpent, slithering and rolling. The cat crawled down

the steps and stumbled under the kitchen window. The pile of dirt next to Fast Eddie's hole began to grow.

Jones awoke in the flower box. When he moved, the pain in his back made him squeak. He dropped into a rhododendron, missed the top branch, and crashed through the leaves to the ground. He kept going as though it had been a perfect landing. The squirrel crept along the foundation. He spotted Puff and crawled toward her.

Fast Eddie sat on the sunflower seed floor. He stared up into the tunnel.

Mr. Plotkin dug deeper.

22

"You LOOK AWFUL," Jones said.

The cat raised her chin. "I have the worst headache," she said, "and a terrible taste in my mouth. I keep smelling burnt bacon."

"I fell off the gutter. I've never done that before." Jones turned so that his back was to the cat. "Can you see blood? I landed on something sharp."

"You have a hole in your fur, but it's not bleeding."

"Ahhhhhhh," Jones groaned. "Is it big?"

"No." Puff closed her eyes. "Do you ever get headaches?"

"Drink some water." Jones pivoted. "By the way, what happened to Fast Eddie?"

Puff's eyes opened wide.

"He got hit by a car?" Jones asked.

"He didn't die last night," Puff gasped. "He's

about to be shot. And I didn't tell him about the gun. I've got to warn him!"

Puff burst through the azaleas and ran down the driveway. She veered across the lawn, plunged through the garden, and dived into the hole by the downspout.

I'll take the shortcut through the barn, she thought.

Jones followed. He didn't know where he was going, but he felt it was important to follow the cat.

Puff jumped the paint cans. She swerved around the mattress and went headfirst into the hole in the corner of the stall. Jones circled the cans and caught up to the cat at the mattress. He was out of breath and his back stung.

Jones dropped into the hole and crawled out into the daylight. Puff was halfway across the lawn. She looked like she was going to lift up into the air, like a kite, and continue free of the earth. Instead she plowed into the tall grass. Jones was right behind.

"Oh no," Mrs. Plotkin said when she saw the two animals.

Someone's ruining my tunnel, Fast Eddie thought. *They can't do that!* The raccoon crawled forward.

Mrs. Plotkin ran through the kitchen and into Kitty. She went over the top of the dog. Her hands came down hard on the wood floor. Her elbows buckled, and her right hip landed next to her hand. Her cheekbone hit the floor last. The dog cowered and cried apologetically.

Mrs. Plotkin's eyes filled with tears. She got up slowly, walked to the refrigerator, and took an ice cube out of the freezer. She held it to her cheek.

In the middle of the field, Puff slammed into the back of Mr. Plotkin's legs.

Sammy saw his father's head fall backward, and his work boots rise up above the grass. He heard a yell, but he couldn't tell what his father said. The shovel went sideways.

Fast Eddie's head emerged into the sunlight. He crawled into the open and sat down at Mr. Plotkin's feet.

23

No ONE MOVED. Mr. Plotkin stared over his knees and leather boots at the large raccoon.

Puff didn't know what she had hit, but it had opened the cut on her head. Blood poured down the white fur and dripped onto her paws.

Jones was underneath the cat. He couldn't see anything.

I'm a raccoon, Fast Eddie thought, *and I'm not running away.*

Mr. Plotkin groped for his gun. "Go away," he screamed. He kicked at the grass, but his heel sank into the field as if it were water. His thigh hit the barrel and he realized the gun was underneath him. "Get out of here!" he yelled. His hands closed on the barrel. He rolled onto his side without taking his eyes off the raccoon.

I have a right to be here, Fast Eddie thought. *I was here first. And I'm not scared of you.*

The shotgun went up in the air. Mr. Plotkin was on his knees behind it.

Two crows in a pine tree stared at the confusion. Their cold faces seemed only mildly interested. One reached down and scratched his chin with his claw. The other frowned.

Fast Eddie looked up the barrel into Mr. Plotkin's right eye. Mr. Plotkin looked down the barrel at a spot between the raccoon's two brown eyes. The blood smeared across Puff's eyes and made the entire scene wavy.

Mr. Plotkin closed his eyes. "AAAAAAAhhhh," he cried.

The crows' wings flapped against their bodies. They lifted off the branch and flew sideways away from the tree. Their feet dangled beneath them.

When Mr. Plotkin yelled, the gun slipped in his hands. His fingers tightened and there was a sharp, deafening bang.

Mrs. Plotkin dropped the ice cube. Sammy covered his eyes and started to cry. A noise came out of Puff's throat that she had never heard before.

When the gun moved, Fast Eddie turned. The buckshot hit him. He felt a burning at the base of his spine. The raccoon pitched forward. His nose and mouth descended through the grass into the dirt. He stared at blackness.

The gun dropped to the ground. The barrel clinked when it hit the blade of the shovel. Mr. Plotkin stood up and stared at the mound of fur and blood. He remembered the first time he'd seen Sammy's blood. The two-year-old hands had grabbed a knife in the dishwasher. Mr. Plotkin had yelled at Sammy. "How could you do that? How could you do that? How could you do that?"

The crows landed in an oak tree. They shifted from side to side and settled into position.

"I knew he'd get it," said one.

"Me, too. Animals never win," grunted the other.

"Will you miss him?"

There was a long silence.

"No," replied the second crow. He leaned forward. "What's he doing?" he asked.

Mr. Plotkin slipped his hands under the raccoon and scooped him up against his chest. He stood up slowly. The striped tail hung by a string. Mr. Plotkin walked quickly toward the barn. The tail swung.

Mrs. Plotkin was sitting on the back steps.

"Get the car door," Mr. Plotkin yelled.

Fast Eddie felt the cold vinyl against his face, but he couldn't move. He listened to the voices:

"Call the vet."

"What?"

"Tell them I'm bringing in a raccoon."

"They don't take raccoons."

"Tell them I'll pay them a lot. I want them to sew a tail on. Talk them into it. They'll need a muzzle and a sedative. Tell them they'll be in the papers. Dr. McKean will do it. What happened to your cheek?"

"Never mind. Just get going. What if he wakes up in the car?"

"I'll drive faster."

Sammy lay down on his bed. He pulled his stuffed dinosaur next to him and looked up at his poster of puppies.

"I hate Dad," he said through his teeth.

24

"Roll over, roll over, roll over," Jones yelled. Puff heard the words, but she didn't know what they meant. The squirrel kicked her in the stomach.

"Oh," the cat grunted. She rolled onto her back.

"I'm lucky you didn't crush me!" Jones gasped. He jumped forward. His paws landed in blood.

"Blood," Jones whispered. "Blood?"

Puff was so tired, she couldn't complain or worry or even feel sad. The words came out in a matter-of-fact way as if she were telling a story about ants.

"It's Fast Eddie's blood. Mr. Plotkin shot him. He hit him and blood went everywhere. Fast Eddie looked like he was dead. Mr. Plotkin picked him up. I heard the car. Fast Eddie's tail was hanging by a piece of fur."

Jones gagged and vomited. There was a sharp pain in his back.

Puff licked her front paw. She closed her eye and wiped the lid with her paw. She licked again.

"I hate the taste of blood," she said.

"Do you think he'll live?" Jones asked. He looked up at the cat. "You have blood all over your head," he added.

Puff wiped her cheek and up into her ear.

"I don't know," she replied.

Mrs. Plotkin sat on the edge of Sammy's bed.

"I don't feel well," Sammy said.

Mrs. Plotkin's fingers patted Sammy's curls.

"Did he kill him?" Sammy asked.

"Rocky may lose his tail, but I think he'll be all right. Dad took him to the vet. Dr. McKean said they're not supposed to take raccoons, but they've done it before. They'll give him lots of shots."

"Why's your cheek purple?" Sammy asked.

Mrs. Plotkin smiled. "I ran into Kitty. Actually, I somersaulted over the top of Kitty."

"Is Kitty okay?"

"Yes, Sammy. Kitty's fine."

For the first time, Fast Eddie was scared. He'd never ridden in a car.

I'm not moving, he thought, *but the ground is.* There was talking and singing, then a click. Mr. Plotkin turned off the radio.

When the car slowed down, the raccoon rolled forward. He slid off the seat and onto the floor. Mr. Plotkin glanced over his shoulder, groaned, and drove faster.

The raccoon stared at a baseball and a small green sock under the front seat. He thought about the full

moon and the mangled mailbox. He felt like he was floating in circles around the moon. Occasionally, he would glance down at the earth and watch a green station wagon driving down a narrow road.

Fast Eddie recognized pain. It had been there all the time, of course, but the raccoon had felt fuzzy and disconnected and he hadn't paid attention. It was a twinge, then a twisting, and finally a digging, grinding pain. It rose up his spine and slid around his brain until he could feel it behind his eyes. *I'm a raccoon,* Eddie said to himself. *I'm a raccoon. I'm a raccoon.*

"You're going to be all right, Rocky," said Mr. Plotkin.

Who's Rocky? the raccoon wondered.

The car stopped and all the doors opened at once. Eddie heard talking, but it sounded like gurgling. A cage went over his mouth and eyes and was strapped to the back of his head.

"The gun went off," he heard Mr. Plotkin explain. "It was an accident."

Fast Eddie felt a sharp stab in his rear leg. Then he fell backward down a tunnel. He passed his lightning bugs and his moss cushions. His rear legs swung by Jones and Puff. He never landed.

"He's out cold," Dr. McKean said. "Let's pick him up."

Dr. McKean and his assistant spent two hours sewing on Fast Eddie's tail. Three days later, they sent Mr. Plotkin a bill for four hundred and seventy-five dollars.

25

THE STATION WAGON pulled into the driveway and coasted to a stop in front of the back-door. Puff sat on a branch in the magnolia tree. Jones lounged in a gutter nearby.

"This could be him," Puff said.

The door opened and Mr. Plotkin climbed out. "Rocky's home," he yelled.

Sammy burst out of the house and ran to the back of the station wagon. He put his hands on the glass and looked inside.

"Wait a minute," Mrs. Plotkin said from the kitchen. "I'll help you lift the cage."

"Cage?" Jones said. "Did you know anything about a cage, Puff?"

The cat didn't answer.

"Are we going to take care of him, Dad?" Sammy asked.

"No," Mr. Plotkin answered. "He's a wild animal, not a house pet. Dr. McKean says he's well enough to go back to his hole. We'll put some food out."

"I can't wait to see him." Mrs. Plotkin walked across the porch and down the steps. "How does he look?" Puff watched blond curls pass beneath her.

"Fine," Mr. Plotkin answered quickly.

The door swung open.

"What's wrong with his tail?" Sammy cried.

"Nothing," Mr. Plotkin said. "It's been operated on. It's only been a week. It'll look better eventually."

"It's not fluffy anymore," Sammy said.

Puff closed her eyes. *Eddie's so proud of his tail,* she thought.

Jones looked at his own tail.

The cage scraped against the door and clanked on the driveway.

Jones leaned over the gutter. "I can't see him," he said. "Mrs. Plotkin is in the way. What does he look like?"

Puff watched the raccoon circle the cage. "He's thinner," she said.

"What about his tail?" Jones asked. "What did they do to his tail?"

The lifeless tail lay behind Fast Eddie. *It used to float,* Puff remembered. The fur was matted and dull. "It looks the same," she said.

"Will it get bigger?" Sammy asked.

"We'll leave chocolate chip ice cream in the trash," Mrs. Plotkin said. "That tail will look better in no time."

"And cinnamon toast," Sammy added.

"What about a steak and some asparagus?" Mr. Plotkin added. "Wouldn't you like that, Rocky?"

"One, two, three, four, five, six," Sammy said. "He has six rings."

"They had to shorten one at the base," Mr. Plotkin explained as he squatted. "Okay. Time to let you go, Rocky. Make sure Kitty's in the house, Sammy."

"Can't I do it, Dad?"

"Go stand on the porch, Sammy. You never know what a wild animal will do."

"Kitty's inside," Mrs. Plotkin said as she climbed up the back steps. She held Sammy's hand. "Go ahead."

The cage door swung open. Mr. Plotkin backed into the daylily bed.

Fast Eddie stepped out of the cage and looked up at Mr. Plotkin. He squinted. A car passed the end of the driveway. Eddie's head turned toward the noise. He

started forward, following his nose toward the road.

"No. No," Mr. Plotkin said.

The raccoon's head was just above the driveway. His tail dragged on the tar.

"Not that way," Mrs. Plotkin yelled.

Puff's claws dug into the bark. Jones's head disappeared.

"He's going to get hit," Sammy screamed.

Mr. Plotkin ran along the grass. He waved his arms over his head and yelled, "SHOO, SHOO."

Fast Eddie moved faster.

Mr. Plotkin yelled, "The field, the field." Mrs. Plotkin and Sammy jumped off the porch.

Mr. Plotkin tried to get in front of the raccoon, but Eddie ran over his sneakers.

A black sedan cruised down the road. The driver's arms were straight and his fists gripped the top of the steering wheel. He never saw the raccoon.

"Just do it, do it, do it," he sang with the voice on the radio.

Fast Eddie didn't hesitate at the end of the driveway. He waddled out to the yellow line and in front of the shiny chrome bumper.

The car purred on down the road.

26

PUFF AND JONES thought that Fast Eddie had been hit by the car. Puff hid beneath the crib in the barn. She stared at the bag of peat moss. Jones crawled through a hole in the gutter and crouched behind a box of Christmas tree ornaments.

Mr. and Mrs. Plotkin thought that the raccoon had been given too much anesthetic during his operation.

"He was confused," Mr. Plotkin said. "He thought he was going toward the field."

"That makes sense," Mrs. Plotkin added.

Sammy thought Rocky was proving how brave he was. Just before the raccoon crawled into the opposite yard, he turned and examined each member of the Plotkin family. Sammy was sure Rocky smiled.

At midnight, Puff stood up and stretched. Her mouth opened wide and her tongue extended and curled. The crib, the barrel of cans, and the mattress blended into the blackness. Puff oozed silently between them. In the corner, she found the hole and squeezed out into the garden.

The moon was gone. The night was thick. The cat proceeded down the driveway toward the road.

Sammy screamed, "NO!"

"He's having a nightmare," Mrs. Plotkin announced. "You'd better plan to sell that stupid gun."

She climbed out of bed. Mr. Plotkin watched the second hand on the alarm clock.

Puff crouched at the end of the driveway. Her tail wrapped around her left side. The end twitched below her chin. She wondered why she couldn't smell blood.

Jones tiptoed along the stone wall. He jumped to the grass, hopped across the tar, and squatted next to Puff. The two animals stared at the yellow line in front of them. Puff thought about the sunflower seed floor. Jones remembered the first time he'd met Fast Eddie.

Lamb chops and orange rinds, Jones thought. *That's what he wished for on the first star.*

Mrs. Plotkin hugged Sammy and whispered, "It's all right. You're just having a nightmare."

"There's no blood," Jones said.

"None?" Puff asked.

"Of course, they could have washed the road. That would be just like the Plotkins."

"We'd still smell it."

"I know," said Jones.

Sammy's arms squeezed Mrs. Plotkin's neck. "Mom . . ." he whimpered. "The gun went off. I was in the way."

"Then he didn't get hit," Puff said.

"Maybe when the car hit him, he went flying. Maybe he's over there behind that stone wall," Jones suggested.

"I'm not a basketball. Honestly, Jones!" said a hoarse voice from the opposite side of the road.

The cat and the squirrel flinched as if the voice had swung at them.

Fast Eddie emerged from the lowest branches of a green bush. He crept out into the road and sat on the yellow line.

"Eddie!" Puff murmured. "You're alive."

"What about your tail?" Jones blurted.

Puff gasped. "It's fine. Your tail will be fine. It takes time for tails to heal. Tails are very slow."

"Dad is going to get rid of his gun, Sammy," Mrs. Plotkin said. "Then you won't have to worry." She pulled up the covers.

"I wish he'd shot it off," Fast Eddie announced.

"What!" Puff and Jones said together.

"It was the best tail I ever saw," Fast Eddie declared, "but I don't need it." He leaned forward and grinned. "People don't have tails, and look what they get away with."

"You're right," Puff agreed. Jones nodded.

"But he didn't shoot it off," Eddie said, "so I have to drag this thing around. It doesn't bother me that much, as long as I don't look at it. I have to pretend it's not there."

"That's a good idea," said Puff.

"Maybe it'll help me out. It should scare off a few dogs, especially when I tell them what happened."

Puff heard a car. She closed her eyes and pulled her tail in closer. The headlights swung across the road as the car turned left and squealed around the corner.

"There's a big world out there," Fast Eddie said, "and lots of barrels waiting to be knocked over. I'm sick of the Plotkins."

"They're so strange," Jones said. "Did you see Mr. Plotkin? He was waving his arms."

"Did you see me go over his shoes, Puff?" the raccoon asked.

"You were fearless," Puff declared.

The raccoon smiled. "You've been a good friend, Puff. My best friend. I won't forget you. Maybe someday I'll come back and tell you what's out there." He turned and started forward along the yellow line. "Don't ever forget me, Puff," he said over his shoulder.

Puff wanted to say, "I won't, Eddie," but she couldn't speak.

The raccoon got smaller and smaller, and disappeared around the corner. Puff knew he'd duck into the woods, but he wanted to be remembered leaving on the yellow line.

"He'll be fine out there," Puff whispered. She sat back on her haunches, lifted her paw, and licked the top side.

"What about you?" Jones asked.

Puff placed her paw on the driveway. "I'll miss the sculptures," she said. "Eddie could do a lot with artichoke leaves. But I'm not a raccoon. I'm looking forward to long naps and peaceful nights. I hated worrying all the time. Having a best friend can wear you out."

"He really showed those Plotkins," Jones said.

Sammy rolled onto his side. "Will Rocky ever come back, Mom?" he asked.

"Maybe someday," Mrs. Plotkin said. "When you're all grown up. You'll know him. He'll be the one with six rings." She turned off Sammy's light and kissed him on the forehead.

"Are you cold?" she asked.

"A little."

Mrs. Plotkin walked over to the window. She pulled up the shade and looked down at the end of the driveway.

If there had been a moon, Mrs. Plotkin would have noticed a white cat sitting next to a red squirrel. She would have remembered seeing the same two animals running into the field just before the gun went off. She would have known that the animals were friends and imagined a crazy story about them.

However, it was a dismal night, and Mrs. Plotkin couldn't see anything. She closed the window halfway and padded down the hall to bed.